Eliza Houk

Puritan, a Poem in Seven Cantos

Eliza Houk

Puritan, a Poem in Seven Cantos

ISBN/EAN: 9783744708227

Printed in Europe, USA, Canada, Australia, Japan

Cover: Foto ©Andreas Hilbeck / pixelio.de

More available books at **www.hansebooks.com**

PURITAN.

A POEM

IN SEVEN CANTOS.

Contents.

PURITAN.

CANTO THE FIRST.

THE VOYAGE.

I.

WHAT quivering craft braves Ocean's stormy deep?
    What daring will bears on in such a gale?
    The boreal winds, fierce, unobstructed, sweep,
The autumnal clouds droop low, and darkly veil
The pointed mast's damp cords and tattered sail;
There, thro' o'erwhelming wave appears the bow!
In wracking trough, a feather were less frail;
The upper works rise torn to fragments now!
Yet onward course she holds, with bold unwavering prow.

II.

Floats there a god that naught on earth can scathe?
Or saddest outcast that dares tread no land;
Or wretched victim of dread sovereign's wrath;
Or one that tempts all ills, haply to strand
Where golden treasure doth such risks demand?
Draw near in awe and wonder! Can it be?
Lo! there behold the hero;—See him stand
In human form, but godlike majesty;
Unawed, unsaddened, calm in perfect faith is he.

2   V

III.

He leans against the creaking mast, and feels
The Ocean's pulse in every trembling beam;
The wind holds him fast bound, and now reveals
Beneath his long dark pilgrim's gown, the gleam
Of sword and corselet; and his eye doth seem
To pierce thro' mists and clouds, and view beyond,
The land of hope and promise; for no dream
The precious words that he but now hath conned;
Tho' wet, wind-torn, each page forbids him to despond.

IV.

Is it responsive to that fervent prayer?
The sun has broken thro' the murky tide
Of ragged clouds, dark fringes trailing bare
Across the blue beyond; now clear descried
In sudden light, his ills seem magnified!—
Was he a hero thus to dare alone?
Behold him thrice heroic; by his side,
His arm around her, clings a fragile one;
Too dear; her every pang far sorer than his own.

V.

Her eyes, a heavenly blue, with his, seek heaven;
In that too sudden brightness, turn again
To rest on him; fond Charitè, God given,
Blessing divine, nor given to him in vain.
How fair and pallid!   Each keen throbbing pain
Her unveil'd temple shows; her sunny hair
Rude, wind-disheveled, her apparel plain,
Lacking its wonted folds, her arms half bare,
Seem strained to save one treasure, no whit safer there.

VI.

It is indeed upon her breast a child!
A tender infant that there knows no fears;
A maid beside, close clinging, wailing wild,
Mingles with Ocean's brine her early tears;
And still a youth, anear the sire appears,
Pale, but unmoved; erect in earliest pride,
He emulates the faith that he reveres;
The storms and ills of earth doth proud abide,
His stubborn will calls God's, and grows self-deified.

VII.

And not afar, the sturdy followers group
Before and aft, some scores seem clustered close;
These too clasp tender treasures. A bold troop,
As ever crossed the Ocean. Is it dross—
A faith that doth the human soul engross
Until it rests all things it holds most dear—
Against all human senses fears no loss—
Trusting a Being that the soul draws near,
Who, to the Spirit's vision, faith—alone is clear?

VIII.

What matters them, if howling tempests roar!
What, if a thousand miles of storming waves
Spread raging either side; behind, before;
What, tho' the lightning midnight blackness paves!
What, tho' the quivering, shattered bark scarce saves
The precious freight of all that mortals prize,
From dreadful plungings to dark watery graves!
What, tho' one dead in their sad vision lies!
Is not their life a pilgrimage, and Heaven the prize?

IX.

The ship is damp and dismal, scattered o'er
With many fragments of the broken deck;
Heard ye that startling cry! Those brave before,
Seized with dismay, their dreadful doom deplore;
Not only are the upper works a wreck,
Amidship's beam is wrenched, what now can check
The wild waves' fatal power! She settles low!
Each wave breaks higher up—a hair—a speck—
As sure as life ebbs out—however slow,
When bright arterial current from a wound doth flow—

X.

So surely that fell stream, still flowing in,
Will still the throbs of full an hundred hearts;
Is there no help? The knight doth hush the din,
The faint gives strength—he hopeful hope imparts,
And hastens on, if haply human arts
May here suffice, God willing, to repair
The fearful vent! " He ne'er his righteous thwarts,
But gives the weak His power, and doth declare
He will bless them that serve Him; wherefore need ye fear."

XI.

Aye, He who knew their future, there had stored
An instrument for e'en this dread hour's need;
Whose aid they never vainly had implored.
With wise and patient labor, they succeed—
The breach repair. From this great danger freed,
Now many stand about him, and implore
Ere certain doom devour them, to relead
Them back to their late haven—to restore,
At least their lifeless forms to that dear native shore.

XII.

Sadly he listened to their sore complaint,

Speechless he waited till they ceased to speak;

And if a tear had gathered, quick restraint

Forbade it damp his dark and furrowed cheek.

For e'en the gentle dame, so worn and meek,

Had prayed him pause; her tender buds to spare,

Where waves grew wilder, and the winds more bleak;

If for an instant touched with others' care,

Unwavering will—his stern unfaltering words declare.

XIII.

"Doth God divide his domain?   Doth His care

But over half the Ocean's waves extend?

Will He, whose mercy hath sufficed each where,

No longer from the raging storms defend?

The sea is His—He made it, and doth send

His breath in winds athwart it, to and fro;

They smite the clouds; hail, snow, and rains descend;

They smite the sea, the waves to mountains grow;

He wills—bright skies—calm seas, make earth with beauty
    glow.

XIV.

"Why are ye here upon this unknown sea?

Did youthful fervor urge a headlong course?

Ye know full well how long and prayerfully

Ye dwelt upon this way; in sage discourse,

How every ill and peril I with force

Did seek portray, that none might venture hence

In weakness, making foul this stream's pure source;

Delays befell, thro' God's good providence,

To winnow out the chaff; who sought a fair pretence

XV.

" Might now at ease on England's shores repose;
Or share their cherished brethren's patient toil,
Within the hospitable realme they chose,
With many exiled from their native soil,
When their fair homes the spoiler joyed to spoil.
Ye chose the better part—ye vowed to find
Some far retreat beyond the world's turmoil,
A refuge for your babes, for they had pined
Like prisoned birds in lands too cumbered, tho' most kind.

XVI.

"A tender foster-mother twelve long years
Hath Holland been; but her own children earned
Within her narrow bounds their bread with tears;
Ye felt the sore constraint; ye, weeping, turned
From sight of your poor children, who had learned
To wear too grave a look, unplayful, wise,
Grown old and weary in that brief sojourn;
Would ye return, cage them again?   They rise
E'en now, their wings will bear at least to paradise!

XVII.

" England to you a poorer refuge far;
Have ye forgotten how ye were a prey
To that proud hierarchy?   They sought to mar
Not only your poor homes, yourselves to lay
In dungeons damp, far from the light of day.
They sought the deathless soul foul to deprave—
With gainful bait entice—sought every way
With fears to force you your own souls t'enslave;
Ye strong, escaped; but what would weaker offspring save?

XVIII.

" England 's no home to you ; a popish king
Hath harrowed you from out her goodly soil ;
But still ye love your native tongue—dared bring
Your treasures on the Ocean—disembroil
Yourselves from her disputes, and freely toil
A noble state in loyalty to found ;
Forget no hope, lest fear may foully foil
A worthy labor ;—and tho' cares abound,
God's grace much more ; e'en o'er this vast unknown Pro-
　　found.

XIX.

" Nor dare ye once reproach my guidance here.
He who dares murmur, tho' deep troubles press
In grievous burdens that he scarce can bear,
Murmurs against his God.   Never distress,
But He hath meted, sinful soul to bless ;
Guiana wooed you with her lavish gold ;
Virginius prayed you join his host no less ;
Mauritius proud, rich gainful trade foretold
About the forts whose future greatness he extolled.

XX.

" I promised naught but grief and poverty ;
As Israel from Egypt, hence I came,
Nor feared the wilderness beyond the sea ;
To rear an altar to His holy name,
Nor brooked one follower zeal did not inflame ;
To fast, to pray, give thanks as seemed me good ;
If any now gainsay, theirs be the shame ;
We came to find pure streams of heavenly food,
To rear our offspring, first of many a goodly brood."

XXI.

He ceased, then breathed a long and fervent prayer,
Nor rose a plaint from e'en an infant there ;
The helmsman with inspired courage held
The prow to West, the wind seemed shifting fair,
The mariners loosed ; the sail slow swaying swelled,
And swift through heaving brine the bark compelled.
It was a fair and gallant sight the while,
From every brow sad weight of care dispelled—
There was no sound of mirth, but many a smile
And pure and calm thanksgiving did the hours beguile.

XXII.

Darkness succeeds the brightest day's sunshine,
Tempests the calm, and nights and storms ensued
Till hope deferred made many a heart repine ;
The knight in faith exalted, unsubdued
By every ill, his soul with grace imbued.
Three score of days upon that troubled sea,
Each added morn no land, each night they stood
Watching the sun, if haply there might be
A shore-line cross the orb,—watching, how longingly !

XXIII.

One, two, aye, three ; each day dawned but on waves ;
Behind, before, each way a dreary sight.
One, two, aye, three ; no ray of sunlight paves
The darkening sea ; passes the pale twilight,
No trace of land appears ere falls the night ;
The morn—the fourth—the earliest dawn on high
Paces a quick impatient path—the knight—
Oft times his searching gaze strained anxiously,
But lingering darkness doth his hope as oft belie.

XXIV.

How keen the northern blast! the spray blown high
Congealing o'er his form; but still he stands
Spell-bound in instant prayer;—"The clouds that lie
Dark on the West—tell me—are they not lands!
Ye mariners behold! the view expands,
The lingering dimness vanishes.—Oh God!
Not unrewarded they, who Thy commands
Obey.   Tho' heavy falls the chastening rod,
We shall tread that near land, as Israel, Canaan trod,

XXV.

" Awed through the middest deep, at length beyond,
Praising the living God, the same Lord then,
To-day, as yesterday—ever in bond
With those who love and serve Him.   Godly men,
When did He once forsake you? tell me, when?"
They gather close around their faithful guide;
Tears, smiles, thanksgivings loud, unseeking ken
What trials wait them there, land! land descried!
Hour of hope realized, elate, o'erjoyed, they ride.

XXVI.

"Bear to the South!" The mandate, helm obeyed;
The voice imperious as the power supreme,
He, unforgetful, tho' enrapt they stayed,
Gazing upon the wished-for shore and dream
To tread firm land, nor breathe they other theme,
But he beholds them shuddering in the blast,
Keen, unrelenting, sweeps it, cold extreme,
And seeks, the long peninsula once past,
For some safe haven where they may find rest at last.

3

XXVII.

But it was vain; he could have borne their grief,
To draw no nearer now that longed-for shore,
But hope for rest that way was sad as brief;
Dread shoals and breakers threatened more and more,
To wreck their shattered ship, and all her store;
The hope of drawing near a friend grew faint,
The hope, of even life 'mid perils sore,
Lost when the wind, attending their complaint,
Veers to the South, forcing them back—God's own con-
    straint.

XXVIII.

A day and night upon that rock-bound coast!
Another morning 'round that yearned-for land!
A headland bold, and narrow, for the most
Dense wooded to the shore—nigh such a strand,
The vast and furious Ocean passed, doth stand
The knight—brave, proud, inspired to lead the van
Of hosts that dared to follow his command,
And in the light of faith unfold a plan
Conceived nor carried out by mortal man—
Needs it proclaim this daring Hero—*PURITÀN.*

PURITÀN.

CANTO THE SECOND.

CELEBRATED VOYAGES.

I.

GREAT Puritàn! How much the world hath writ
    Of famous voyages o'er Oceans vast!
  With jealous care the ancients sought transmit
  E'en dim traditions of exploits long past,
  When daring mariners shrank back aghast
  From fearful perils in the fair Levant;
  Ere man conceived what mighty depths were massed
  Beyond his knowledge. Care most vigilant,
Has failed one labor find, as thine significant!

II.

  But lest strange unbelief the truth may scorn,
  And deem such hero-worship, weak, unwise,
  Deeds of renown, that earliest adorn
  Th' historic page, or that men doubly prize
  Where poets give immortal fame, arise!
  In order show your valiant; tell them o'er,
  E'en fables of pelagic enterprise;
  Nor shrink ye sages, and the task deplore;
Is it not worthy to record such deeds once more?

III.

Bold Argonautica! be yours the praise
Of earliest glory on the untried deep;
Tho' trade of spicery in earlier days
Allured the prow, the fragrant gain to reap
Far down th' Arabian sea—perchance to creep
Eurythrean currents thro' for pearls and gold,
Rich gains were theirs, the glory thou may'st keep,
Oh princely Jason! chief of heroes old;
Patron of Argus, thro' all time how oft extolled!

IV.

Yet only left he Thessaly, to touch
The Isle of Lemnos; thence to Mysia cross,
Lingering in Thrace to learn what needed much
The dread Symplegades, without a loss
Pass thro'—tho' wrathfully they clash and toss,
And then the Euxine sea, vast as unknown,
Sails—labored oars compelled them far across
To Colchis come—the golden fleece he won
Thro' wise Medea's love. Such aid 'twere well to shun.

V.

Thence back to Thessaly, saving the two,
Hylas and Hercules, whom friendship stays
On Mysia's shore—again Alcides view,
This but a boyish deed, when he obeys
Command Eurystheus gave to steer where graze
Geryon's famed oxen; Erytheia's day
Dawned far to West—he dared the sunset rays,
Seeking Hesperides, where guarded lay
The golden apples that he sought to bear away.

VI.

In monumental grandeur stands it now,
Unfallen not unchanged, the riven pass
Of Hercules! His labors famed avow
The starry heavens, where fadeless glories glass
The deeds that earthly monuments surpass;
Here pass'd too, Menelaüs, world renown'd,
As spouse of Helen, too fair cause, alas!
Of Troy's sad fall; and this beyond the bound
Of sage Ulysses' wanderings, whose griefs astound.

VII.

Æneas' voyage recall, who bravely bore
His sire Anchises from the wreck of Troy,
To found far o'er the seas, on presaged shore,
Another state, to be a pride and joy
Greater than that just lost—without alloy
The deep delights the poet gives the soul
Where e'en the ancient gods he dares employ,
To lend a lustre that exalts the whole,
That scarce Ulysses' tale the ages more extol.

VIII.

But leave we song and fable, for we find
Not here, one purpose worthy place beside
The high, soul-daring, heaven-exalted mind
Of this our hero—glory, human pride,
Nor knowledge, much less love and faith sore tried!
But seek we now the old historic tomes
If haply there the truth may best abide,
Seleucus, Alexander Magnus roams,
Patrocles—Onesecritus, none worthy comes.

IX.

And leave we these few annals of renown;
For on that bright and placid inland sea
There can no daring deed be truly shown
Worthy compare with Ocean's jeopardy.
There Asia Minor, Greece, and Italy,
Face Egypt, Cyrenecia, Carthage famed
And Spain, tho' far from Palestine it be,
The later mariners no glory claimed,
Save where the boundless seas their fearless zeal inflamed.

X.

'Tis told that Menelaüs was the first
Who passed the cape Speranza, till he came
 To Indies' shores: next Solomon athirst
For golden treasures, mighty ships did frame
To pass the straits of Mecca—riches, fame,
Three years of absence from the East, they brought;
The worthy deed lends lustre to his name;
Then Neco, Egypt's king, in wisdom sought
To join the Red Sea and the Nile, and him bethought,

XI.

Phœnecians wise to send from Mecca down
To dread Speranza, thence to Hercules,
And thence to Egypt; won they great renown
But nothing found their sovereign's hopes to please.
And these same annals tell a favoring breeze
Bore Carthaginian merchants on and on
Ever to westward, thro' tempestuous seas,
 'Till far as our Antilles they had gone,
Six hundred years before the Christian era's dawn.

XII.

When Roman power had reached the far off coast
Of famed Britannia, thro' the Ocean sea,
It was the mighty Empire's proudest boast,
And marks the time her eagle gloriously
Swept to the zenith, and there seemed to be
E'en to the farthest seeing, like a star
Eternally transfixed; laboriously
His pinions all the while unequal are
To stay his sudden downfall; falls he fearful far!

XIII.

Then came the time when all those cultured shores,
Greece, Italy, Gaul, Spain, and Africa,
Were wild with tumults—Vandals, Huns, Goths, Moors,
Sweeping in counter currents; nations saw
Barbaric hordes descend, their glories draw
Swiftly and hopeless to untimely end.
Wide-spreading carnage, plundering might sole law;
No more the richly laden fleets may wend,
No more romantic rivals on the seas contend.

XIV.

In grief we turn away, and let the pall
Of silence o'er such desolation fall;
Barbarian ravages served well to hide
Worse than Barbarian crimes—less tragical
More fatal ills destroyed that vaunting pride;
As came the tempted fierce barbarian tide
Rose grim despair, the stern extreme resource
Of fallen greatness—glory deified
After this fatal lesson!—mark its course
The mighty Roman Empire in the dust a corse,

XV.

It, like the fabled Phœnix, sprang to life;
From cradling sepulchre, arose unseen,
But unlike that fond wonder, from fell strife
Bore not the parent nest—selfish we ween
Hath human glory from the earliest been—
Full plumed and proud emerged it in the West,
Where armoured heroes gathering were seen;
As brilliant birds the stranger phœnix press'd,
So there King Arthur and his Knights, glory attest.

XVI.

Ancient renowned, chivalrous Arthur! thou,
Thou wert the first that dared the northern blast
For conquest, as thy knights impelled the prow,
(Heroic as the Argo bore time past)
From Celtic isle to North, until thou wast
In sight of Hecla's flames; that island bound
To faithful homage, far off Russe at last,
The Norse and Flanders thine, "chambers first found
To Brittain "—bold exploit of the famous Table Round.

XVII.

Wild but heav'n-blest Crusades new life had giv'n
To listless nations; men went to and fro
Doing great deeds of valor—they had striv'n
On land and sea, yearning yet more to know
Of distant parts; the human currents flow
Restless, chivalrous, thro' surrounding seas,
And neighboring countries felt unwonted glow
Of new regard and tender sympathies,
Too soon, alas! disturbed by glory's votaries.

XVIII.

But love, a motive that doth seldom lead
To unknown lands, because the fragile fair
Await in ease until the daring speed
In quest of glory, and if joys are there,
Their tender loves they later thither bear—
Yet once the fatal cause, for unknown shores
Received two lovers in their keen despair.
Too tardy refuge—tho' there lavish stores
Of beauties bloom—one fading beauty he deplores.

XIX.

She died—his love, his life; and unto him
Naught in the skies above, or seas around,
Or riches of that virgin isle, but dim,
More deathful than the narrow precious mound
That all the hopes of his sad soul embound;
Oh joy! the island's hero slept as well;
In stormless haven, love with joy was crowned!
Sad followers mourned in paradise to dwell;
They framed a float, o'erjoyed escaped this tale to tell.

XX.

Near Lusitania heard it not in vain.
Don Henry yearned exalt his native land.
His wise unrivalled zeal gave her the main,
Adown dark Afric's shores; his sails expand,
Until the fiery rays naught can withstand.
Columbus sought the Lusian monarch then,
His mighty project told at his command.
The East to East, sole hope of wisest men;
Faith in the great unseen, when will ye conquer, when?

4

XXI.

To sail to West o'er Ocean was a scheme
Consigned to scorn in ignominious pride.
Then turned the slighted hero—his fond dream
Never dispelled, tho' all the world deride,
Again t' explain tho' Spain as well denied;
The Queen, more wise, his earnest suit attends;
Palos—vast Ocean—Western land descried!
Oh mighty exploit! all the past it shends,
And none save Puritàn's, such vast results portends.

XXII.

De Gama yearned repair the Lusian loss
Of Western Empire, and with constant zeal
Bore on and on the burning line across—
The shores of Afric past, what ills reveal!
The blazing flash! the wracking thunder's peal!
Where mighty waves in counter currents sweep—
Amid such perils pulsing veins congeal,
To pass where "Spirit of the Cape" would keep
Man from all knowledge of that wild and secret deep.

XXIII.

But tho' he gave the coveted, famed East,
With all its kings and kingdoms scarcely seen
To his far monarch, year by year decreased
That empire's fame—for fell ambition keen,
Too ravishing hath in all ages been.
Save freights of gold and purple, spices rare,
Rich freights men prize of luxuries terrene,
And that it roused the daring everywhere,
And of it Camoëns wrote, the world the deed might spare.

XXIV.

While England grieves Columbus, Cabot steers
Straight for the West; St. George floats proudly there
As he the shores, his " Prima vista" nears;
It needs but see the fruitful coast each where,
Down from the north with spreading sails to bear,
Where keenest glimpse commands the dim coast line,
All, all with zeal for England they declare,
The title for the continent consign;
A strange and unreal right that nations must define.

XXV.

France, tardier than her compeers, felt a pang
That none her *Fleur-de-lis* transplanted, where
The world in praise of wealth and glory rang;
Then in her service Verrazanni dare
Her arms across the middest Ocean bear,
To plant them on that coast from South to North
In spacious harbors; he, the earliest there—
But none survive, nor any blooms put forth,
Save where the care of Cartier attends their growth.

XXVI.

Fair Italy! thy sons for others guide
The venturous prow, in far and famous Seas,
Past lands of untold beauty, constant glide;
Yet not one rood of all the loveliest leas
Where soft waves fall, no island galaxies,
No spot of all the New Worlds found, give thee;
Nor bring e'en treasures back thy pride to please;
And thou must see Rome's single legacy,
The fervor of thy sons, enhance thy jeopardy!

XXVII.

And yet how beautiful! Nature and Art
Bedeck thy form with lavish loveliness,
As if to soothe the pangs thy broken heart
Feels, that thy sons degenerate confess
No filial ardor in thy deep distress;
As mourn'd Penelopè her mighty spouse
When suitors arrogant for favors press,
So thou; yet she had her Telemachus;
Wasting thy people's treasures, kings carouse;
When will Ulysses come to frustrate their false vows?

XXVIII.

But haste we to recount a few, the best
Of Ocean's heroes;—bold Magellan sought
To compass this great Earth; he onward pressed
Thro' his famed fret, in middest ocean brought
To untimely end, by savage imps untaught.
Successful Cano, bearing westwardly
That unsought glory through great suffering found;
His monarch proud that all the world might see,
Wrote "*Primus omnium circumdedisti me*"

XXIX.

Upon his shield; and set the globe beneath;
A vaunting emblem, highest boast of fame.
Now scores of mariners their deeds bequeath
Succeeding ages—yet from us scarce claim
'Tho' more deserving—e'en a passing name.
Cabral—Vespucius—Cortereal—Pinzon
Frobisher—Davis—Chancellor o'ercame
The frozen seas, while to the South had gone
Drake, and those bold compeers we blush to dwell upon.

XXX.

In weariness we pause; once more attest
The Knight supreme; yet know Virginius rare
Of England's former màrine heroes best,
And tho' so worthy fame, can he compare
With him we vaunt? forget not, pride did share
Each noblest purpose; glory the high prize
For which the stormy deep he erst did dare,
Later for human rights, did death despise—
Daring alone—for earth and earthly things was wise.

XXXI.

But Puritàn felt no chivalrous pride;
No hope of conquest, no desire of gain;
He sought to worship God—and to abide
His will on earth, in Heaven a rest attain.
He trusted Him he served, in faith was fain
All that he prized, to launch on stormiest main.
Tho' no Shekinah led the unknown way,
Faith unassisted mourns not, death, nor pain,
Nor any labor; he but yearns to pray—
Past fervent youth, young manhood's hardier day,
In Liberty and peace, where none can him gainsay.

PURITÀN.

THE LANDING.

I.

IT is indeed a wilderness;—the shore,
  The sea, hushed, deep, primeval solitudes;
The winter winds o'er wastes of waters roar,
Grey shifting clouds portend the fiercer moods
Of gathering storms—the low dark circling woods
Of sombre cedars, and of shrunken pines,
With sapless boles, mark frigid latitudes;
So chill and silent, that the darksome lines
Of great leviathans, he o'er the waves defines.

II.

And in the bay's deep sheltered close recess,
The myriad fowls have found secure retreat;
Sole animated objects, to possess
Vast silent wilds of nature; region meet
The purposes of Puritàn; replete
With deepest sorrow, he mourns not the pain;
A thousand leagues from friends, from foes deceit
As well dissevered, from the love of gain,
The churchman's pride, and hated papacy's foul chain.

(xxvii)

III.

Thus finds he here, as every faithful breast,
Somewhat for deep thanksgiving e'en amid
Perplexity and care; for those distressed,
The young and fragile; yet the shores forbid—
Within their friendly arms securely hid—
The Ocean's storms disturb their welcome rest.
A thousand ships might float of dangers rid,
Within the great round bay, and some attest
Great shoals of fishes it at certain times possessed

IV.

The growth of trees, e'en to the waters, told
The shore was rich and fruitful, had it been
In any moon save when November cold
Permitted not prepare for winter keen;
Three long, long months of dreary cold, between
Those damp dark days, and earliest cheer of Spring;
Not e'en a hut his tenderest pledge to screen
From snows and icy storms, tho' they shall fling
The fiercest shafts upon them, that such climates bring.

V.

He saw it all—aroused his soul's deep power
Over impending perils, and weak fears;
With zeal heroic to improve the hour;
"Free men, I charge you, hear!" and quick appears
Each faithful follower that his will reveres;
"Freemen of England, know I led you here
To make you doubly free—ye all are peers;
From despot's power ye fled, your purpose dear,
All power here is yours, each marks his own career.

VI.

" The lands before you choose, plant where you will,
For me and mine it is enough to aid
Your labors, and if offspring mine instill
Base counsels by usurping passion swayed,
Be he accursed, his manhood's strength decayed;
Here is set forth my purpose and intent;
Hark ye the scroll—is it in aught gainsaid?
Then let it be a solemn covenant
That will the most discordant elements cement.

VII.

" Let every member of this compact feel,
His duty singly as before his God;
Let each to each be bound, the common weal
First care of all, and charge them sway the rod
The best and wisest, they who zealous plod
Most for the common good; and mark ye well,
Give not nor take offense; ye who have trod
Rough ways together, strive in peace to dwell;
Be wise, and ye shall rear a freeman's citadel.

VIII.

" Ye are no pampered lordlings, to deplore
Lost ease; ye from the earliest learned to bear
Your own and others' burdens; tho' yon shore
Is icy, bleak, ye can all needs repair,
Inured to labor, now no labor spare;
And what the coast denies ye can produce
By corresponding zeal, and toil and care;
What is denied has providential use
To rouse your sleeping powers and energy infuse.

5

IX.

"Know, human wills, if unrestrained, will bring
　Their own best purposes to ill fruition;
　Then in calm moments let wise measures spring
　To bear such stable fruits, that no transition
　Of stormy passions, no turmoiled condition
　Can break the bonds of constituted laws;
　There ever will be many whose ambition
　'Twill be to stand for wise and righteous cause;
He who would disannul, dishonored let him pause!

X.

"He who hath made the Heavens and the Earth,
　The springs, the rivers, seas, all watery deeps,
　Whose providence forbids one moment's dearth
　Of goodly moisture, He earth verdant keeps,
　That man in season, fitting nurture reaps;
　May He so guard and guide you in your ways,
　With spirit and with power, o'er stormiest steeps
　And tempting meads, your pilgrim hearts to raise
Ever to Heaven, your goal, your rest; His be the praise."

XI.

Now yearned he tread the near encircling shore,
　The ship lay deep and tranquil, but the sands
　Forbade approach too near; one effort more,
　Deep wading to the middle, and he stands
　Sole lord of all those wild uncultured lands.
　He marks the sandy hillocks, like the downs
　Of Holland; and his grateful heart expands,
　When he beneath the seeming barren mounds,
Finds rich, deep, hopeful soil to wisely cultured grounds.

XII.

Onward he presses, and too soon beholds
The wide, wide Ocean; this a narrow tongue
Of land; from that low eminence unfolds
A double prospect of wild waves, among
These depths, this friendly arm hath seeming flung
Its verdant length far thro' the sea, to form
A refuge for the knight, whose heart was wrung
By Ocean's wrath, in fleeing earthly storm;
How long since nature 'gan that tender task perform!

XIII.

The trees grew disencumbered, saving where
The rope-like vines clung pendant from on high;
The oak, the ash, the gainful saffras there,
The birch, and walnut, deep green hollies **vie**
With pines and cedars, that refreshingly
Brighten the wintry prospect; draws the day
Darkly, but hopeful to its close; supply
Of fragrant juniper he bears away;
To-morrow their first Sabbath dawns to rest and pray.

XIV.

How many times the earth had turned that bay
Toward the sun,—perfecting year by year
The circumjacent shores. Was this the day?
Did all that long progression center here,—
Doth Nature pause the spirit to revere?
At midnight hour the wind had ceased to blow;
The earth grew silent as the hemisphere
Of stars above it; e'en the water's flow
Was still'd; the mirror'd stars were perfect stars below.

XV.

If Nature waken'd when the sunlight shone,
Her solemn reverence hushed every sound;
The silent rays pervade the air alone;
No cloud strayed o'er the blue expanse that bound
The hallow'd bay and all the shores around;
No wild bird spread its wings to stir the air,
Vast flocks in secret covert on the ground,
Like dry, wind-gathered leaves; the fishes there,
As still, as deep, deep down, the countless pebbles were.

XVI.

What perfect rest it was; the past was past;
The future lay beyond the night to come;
First Sabbath—of a length'ning chain to last
Long as the nation's welfare,—linking fast
The souls of men,—too prone from faith to roam—
To an eternal, spiritual home.
The spirit seemed to brood upon the place:
The calm of trustful love, and all the sum
Of promised blessings swelled each soul with grace;
Pure new-born hopes, and high resolves all fears efface.

XVII.

The Sabbath pass'd, next morn dawned on a scene
Of earnest energy, propitious sign
Of sure success, the shallop lay between;
A score of sturdy men, they form the line,
And low she settles on the shallow brine.
The strong, the weak and weary bear ashore,
Oh blest relief! to those close ships confine;
Tho' wet, and cold, and weary, none deplore;
The dreadful ocean passed, they tread firm land once more!

XVIII.

But Puritàn, impatient all delays,
Waits not the injured shallop to repair;
In weight of armor clad, he sought far ways
For some fair spot where they might best prepare
For coming winter—this his earliest care;
It needs not tell what painful paths he trod,
Seeking the swift and treach'rous natives there,
Up rugged hills, thro' tangled vales to plod,
With painful step and slow, the wet half frozen sod.

XIX.

His armor rent and tarnished, scant repose
He found, where in some thicket he was fain
Kindle the tardy blaze, that struggling rose
Thro' frosts and dampness; but at last to gain
Sight of a haunt that had been, and much grain,
Yellow and precious as pure sands of gold,
Where it had been deep buried from the rain,
By late fled natives, was a joy untold—
O'er flesh and fowl and living springs, he did behold.

XX.

The wondrous river, with heap'd sands between,
Where fairy-like canoes lay on the shore,
He reached at length; had there his shallop been
He might with ease its farthest bounds explore;
But he must weary trace his footsteps o'er,
Across deep valleys reach the fair fresh lake,
Pass bleak, broad highlands, thro' deep woods once more,
Dense, wild, and pathless, he did painful make
His way to where o'er path of sand the slow waves break.

XXI.

When far they heard his arms resounding tell
The wonted signal, they swift bore across
The stormy bay, strong oars the bark impel,
'Tho' rains fall fast, and waves them wildly toss,
Sole thought to reach the knight their souls engross;
Welcome as weary reached the cape at last,
He safe restored, they feared no sorer loss;
Cheering their hearts, he told of lands late pass'd,
Of wealth of corn, of fields but needing seed to cast

XXII.

Into the cultured ground.   All ready now,
The shallop fairly manned, he would them lead
That they might view the land; how rudely blow
The boreal blasts! their only anchor freed,
The winds and waves forbid so rash a deed!
They seek the nearest harbor, there abide
Safely the sweeping storm, but dire the seed
Of fatal ills those snows and ices breed;
Another day more calm they onward ride,
To where dark branching streams the heaped up sands divide.

XXIII.

Some led he inland, while the shallop lay
Along the shore; but soon they wearied there;
The hills were steep, the valleys deep each way
Thro' heavy snow, slow wading everywhere,
Till he to urge their course did kind forbear;
Beneath low pines reposing, chill the night,
The earliest morn they northwardly repair,
To seek the spot where erst had been the knight,
His promised stores of grain their anxious souls delight.

XXIV.

For now they had enough, new fields to plant,
Intending to restore its worth again
In various trinkets, which the natives want.
Thankful their faithful searchings were not vain,
Beneath the frozen soil, that they were fain
With their good swords to hew; now some forsake
The knight, so worn and weary, would constrain
Him to return. He bids them straightway take
Their precious freight, without him their first harbor make.

XXV.

Graves! Graves! how many graves lay on the coast;
Most fair and kindly furnished, as if those
Crumbling to dust, the low or high, might boast
The power to use the arms or wares they chose
When roused up from that deep profound repose;
And not the dark dread savage dead alone,
His searchings well known instruments expose,
The fair light locks of kindred peoples shown
Amid spoiled trinkets, dust, decay, and mouldering bone.

XXVI.

As everywhere, were life and death anear:
Here native huts, or rather bowers, meet
More gentle natures—tender saplings rear,
And at the middle bent with art discreet,
In order ranged, secure and warm and neat
By double hangings of well woven mats,
Rude trenches there, where seethe they savage meat,
With earthen vessels, divers wooden vats
And store of cunning baskets, and unfinished plaits.

XXVII.

Nor lacking ornaments: the great stag horns
Fastened conspicuous, with eagle's claws,
And hoof of deer, where silken grass adorns
The walls—parched acorns, fishes fit for maws
Of such wild imps—with much that sadly draws
Pained thoughts of perils; rusted, broken things
From wrecks, or murdered wanderers' stores, give cause
For cautious watchings; far off echoings
Announce the shallop, quickly to the shore he springs.

XXVIII.

How grieved was Puritàn! for well he knew
No proper site was found; day after day
Was passing, cold and colder winter grew;
Now night and coming storms brooked no delay;
The ready wind, transported o'er the bay,
Bearing to their first landing at the cape—
His followers would return the self-same way,
To settle there, from farther pains escape;
But Puritàn was still intent new course to shape.

XXIX.

That harbor true was good, fields ready cleared,
And store of whales, and site somewhat secure,
And tho' the coming winter's storms he feared,
When they must dig and build, the while endure
Ice, snows, and biting winds, and sadly sure,
More scant provisions must them ill sustain;
But here low waters were e'en now impure,
Brought far up rugged hills, with sorry pain;
Might there not lie anear some fair well watered plain?

XXX.

One told of far Angoam, one had been
Upon these shores before, and knew a place
Where coursed a noble river, headlands green,
Enclosing Ocean's waves, a goodly space;
He straight advised them once more dangers face,
And all the shore with stern resolve retrace.
The hardiest, man the shallop, tho' the cold
Congealed their pulsings in its hard embrace;
He guides the prow, beyond the sands they hold,
Tho' mail of ice like steel their stiffened limbs enfold.

XXXI.

Nigh half a score of leagues, nor wished for sight
Along the shore, of harboring bay or creek;
At length a cove he sees; but for the night
Stays not—more stirring ventures he doth seek,
Intent with yonder savage troop to speak.
They mark him not, sore laboring to secure
Some what unweeted, yet how timid, weak—
Seeing the knight afar, some covert sure
They find in forest shade, or whelming hosts procure.

XXXII.

Despite the shallows he attains the land.
The morrow some to guard the craft remain,
The rest he leads t' explore on either hand,
The narrow bay, yet seeks he far in vain,
A goodly site or savage haunt to gain.
All is deserted, and the great black bulks
Of stranded grampus', dead along the main,
Make yet more drear the prospect, like the hulks
Of broken vessels—far the treacherous savage skulks.

6

XXXIII.

As sank the sun, he turned from ill reward
Of empty huts and cumbering graves, to find
The expected shallop; but the sands retard
Its coming, and with undiscouraged mind,
So late for that hard toil sore disinclined,
They fell the damp and frozen boles to warm
Their stiffened limbs, but scarcely well reclined,
The midnight stillness startling, cries to arm,
Broke through the dismal darkness with intense alarm.

XXXIV.

The blinding redness of the flickering flame,
Made doubly dark the deep encircling wood.
He, watching, passed the danger; dawning came,
Their prayer forgotten never—first best good—
In the dark twilight, some too listless stood,
While others neared the shallop—as the cry
Of the wild natives, in their fiercest mood,
Broke on his ear; his helmet clasped—his eye
Ranges the copse, and marks the unsparing foe too nigh.

XXXV.

His goodly armor thwarts their careful aim;
The swift shafts fly from out the screening trees;
Assurance of the shallop's safety came
To cheer his heart; his hardy followers seize
The blazing match, and mark his enemies,
Till, as the darkness vanished, vanished they;
Not one there wounded, tho' thick strown he sees
Their fallen arrows, dread intent to slay,
With points of brass and bone and eagles' claws alway.

XXXVI.

Time presses, once again upon his way,
He guides along the coast.   Two score of miles,
He onward bears for harboring stream or bay,
Tho' chilly rainings drench, and other whiles
The blinding snow the craft in ridges piles.
And now the rising wind portends worse ills;
The waves break rudely, and no hope beguiles
Of welcome harbor, but with stubborn will
He holds the helm, his earnest purpose to fulfill.

XXXVII.

Strongly he holds it, but the waves more strong
Snap it asunder; then brave ready arms
Seize the firm oars, and sweep the bark along.
Higher and higher rise the waves, sore harms
Them threat, the coming night awakes alarms;
The anxious mariners quickly loose the sail,
The favoring winds may bear beyond the storms;
It swells—they fly a moment on the gale—
The mast bends creaking in the wind's wild wail—
Then like a reed in sunder riv'n, aye! stout hearts quail.

XXXVIII.

The shallop labored deep, but bore along
Upon the raging flood; had human aid
Prevailed, she had been lost dread shoals among;
Safely swift course thro' fearful dangers made,
Within the harbour periled coursing stayed;
Gone helm and sail and mast—to Him alone,
The God of Mercy, whom the knight obeyed,
Be deep thanksgiving that the craft was thrown
Mid rocks and darkness on the sands of shores unknown.

XXXIX.

All thro' that rainy night, tho' weary worn,
They fearful of the treacherous natives, keep
An anxious watch; untrusting fears are born
Of human weakness; Faith had given sweet sleep,
But mid perplexing ills, thus pressing deep
How soon the heart forgets the strength it needs!
The morn disclosed an island—circling sweep
Protecting waves on every side.   He speeds
It o'er; all tenantless the woods and narrow meads.

XL.

Secure from savage spying, 't was a rest
Welcome as needed, and the livelong day
They seek the bark of snow and ice divest,
Their chief's worn tarnished armor bear away
To dry and burnish; tho' its clasps display
No bands of shining metals, 't was a task
Needed and grateful.   Here they tranquil lay
The Sabbath, worship, and God's blessing ask,
Tho' dark the days, in sunlight of his love can bask.

XLI.

Ever in holy rest the Sabbath spent,
Each morrow much refreshed, some noted deeds
Betokened strength enhanced—inspired intent.
The harbor fit for shipping; straight he leads
To land.   Oh! may he find the hav'en he needs.
The shallop nears the extending point of rocks,
About the cliff more warily proceeds,
He springs a-shore; earth's crust has yielded blocks
For firm, unfalt'ring footing, spite the world's rude shocks,

XLII.

How yearns man mark the swift events of time
In matter most enduring, that he deems
Changeless, imperishable, in each clime!
The fond and sad device befitting seems
His fleeting life, unreal as flitting dreams;
Unnumbered generations pass away,
The earth with ruins of their labor teems;
When fond posterity would homage pay
They seek some sure memorial, where all things decay.

XLIII.

Places of earth, where famous deeds were done,
Or siteless areas of once turmoiled seas,
Why are ye honored? why do pilgrims shun
Fair scenes of earth, the daintiest tastes to please,
To seek some shrine whose long lost sanctities
Have left but ruins—mount, or cave, or plain,
A shore, a ROCK, or gnarled and sapless trees,
To mark what has been?   Here they seek to gain
Gleams of th' Invisible, tho' naught but these remain.

XLIV.

The realms of mind and spirit, far more real
Than e'en the granite rocks, that human eyes
Think real to look upon; with hands to feel
Whose very matter changes as time flies;
Oh! may the soul hereafter, say ye wise!—
The heaven-born soul these subtleties attain?
The depth, and influence, as realities
Enjoy—of every onward step they gain,
Who in this earthly life encumbered truth make plain.

XLV.

Ye who are wrapt in matter, bound in clay,
Go hence, and view enthused a trodden STONE,
Where Puritàn's worn footsteps stayed that day!
All else has passed beyond you; that alone
Yet not unchanged, as fond memorial shown;
But ye philosophers, behold his soul
Transfuse a nation's being—seed there sown,
Of lofty principles, have subtly grown,
Until his spirit animates the whole,
And will, with fruits of liberty, while time shall roll!

XLVI.

Children of men! ye are immortal, all!
Ye people this material universe;
Your airy spirits tread this earthly ball
Held here by weight of matter—laws rehearse
How greater forms all lesser bulks coerce.
Your senses are adapted to enjoy
The beauteous things about you, forms diverse,
To frame of crudest matter, to employ
Life's span to better earth, and purge the soul's alloy.

XLVII.

Give then the spirit respite; let it feel
Its strong affinity with things unseen.
Teach it to know the spiritual real;
Its love from things of earth seek ye to wean,
Immortal hopes from earthly hopes to glean;
All matter must decay, then love it not.
The earth itself must perish, what hath been
Is now no more, or changing; time allot
To dwell on heavenly things, pure joys ye scarcely wot.

XLVIII.

And most of all, for most of pain is there,
Love not the spirit's tenement too well;
The rainbow lives a moment, tints most rare
Of sunset skies, how fitfully they dwell
Upon the vision! Harmonies may spell,
But listening—fade forever from the ear;
And pleasures far less transient these excel,
Pure subtle joys to every sense most dear,
But sure as rainbows fade, and bright skies disappear,

XLIX.

So sure these forms must perish; let the heart
Love first the source of spirit-life—its God.
And then of earthly treasures, love the part
That cannot perish—let the immortal plod
The path of life, and strive to make its clod
A beauty and a blessing—yet to feel
Content to lay it low beneath the sod,
When heaven recalls the spirit; Oh! the weal
Of perfect faith in all that God doth here reveal.

L.

It was a joy to find sweet running streams;
Fair fields expanding, aye, a goodly site;
No more he cared to view—these precious gleams
Of hope, he yearned convey soon as he might,
To those dear anxious ones, from whose fond sight
So many days dissevered—glad to lead
The great ship thence. Tho' cruel ills affright,
They disembark on that cold shore ; hearts bleed
As frail and tender footsteps o'er its ices speed.

PURITAN.

CANTO THE FOURTH.

RETROSPECT.

I.

WHO said it was the Morning Star that shone,
    Rousing the nations for the coming light ?
Fallacious, fond belief; thick clouds had thrown
A dense, dark veil, athwart the dome of night;
There was no force, that with resistless might
Could tear the blackness, till at the very noon
Of utter night; then heav'nly beams grow bright,
And thro' the shrinking vapors shine the moon
And long-prevented stars: with Heaven man may commune

II.

But the same Power that swept the clouds away,
Revealing to the wakeful, wished-for light,
Gathered the folds again, and stayed each ray,
However fitful, from the earth's deep night;
Welcome the many, darkness; men delight
To slumber, calmly, trusting watchmen lone,
Where on the towers they strain the weary sight.
How black the zenith, where the orbs late shone!
North, South, West, East, a dark close smothering horizon

III.

Those watchmen died, successors passed away,
　But those who stood the time, did see the Star,
The Morning Star! paled by the coming day!
　Tho' the unrisen Sun was still afar,
　Ever, less bright, the glowing glories mar
Its shining.　Now the whiteness purples; grows
　The band of brightness, crowding clouds would bar
　The glory, but the earth rolls on! how glows
The ruddy East!　The darkest clouds bright rays enrose—

IV.

Bright, all their varied points and edges, thrown
　Against dark depths in glowing almandine;
The atmosphere along the earth, quick shone
　With light, as gorgeous as thro' ruddy wine;
　The fearful 'gan dread portents to divine,
The blood red orb rose vast, dire mortal strife
　Presaging; high the sun, in hyaline,
　Pure, azure depths, the snowy clouds were rife;
Beneath such skies, earth was astir with busy life.

V.

The clouds had screened awhile the mountain heights,
　But soon evanishing to azure air,
Disclosed their dazzling snows; reflected lights
　Brightened the land around, and every where
　Brought charms to life beneath the glorious glare;
As well intensest contrast;—shadows deep,
　Frigid, eternal, darksome, ever there;
　But fair the silent lakes reflect each steep,
Sunlit or dark, pure forms they sternly strive to keep.

VI.

But what of PURITAN! forefathers his
Were watchmen darkest nights; the moon, each star,
Had seen; the sleepers roused from lethargies,
'To watch the expected dawn tho' clouds it mar,
And kept them wakeful, when it seemed afar;
When rose the burning orb, they strong and stern,
Welcomed presaging dangers; peace or war
Alike to them; the day had dawned, return,
Should such night never; tho' themselves for torches burn.

VII

The night had had its uses; tho' the earth
It had in darkness shrouded, making man
To stumble, blind; giv'n dang'rous errors birth,
Confusing human senses; to their ken,
It had celestial things made brightest then,
Had lured their spirits upward, free to gaze
On glories, else perchance to denizen
Of earth forever lost; but these ne'er raise
Their anxious, willful eyes, they seek for naught to praise.

VIII.

They were the type for martyrs; they could see
Naught good in that which they had learned to hate;
Nor trust e'en virtue in an enemy;
To die was nothing; 'twas a welcome fate,
Rather than what they held as truth, abate
One jot.   'Gainst earthly powers they fearless turned,
Patient to perseveringly await
Their time; if need be peace or life they spurned;
Death pangs to such tried faith had untold numbers earn'd.

IX.

There was a scroll they long had known divine;
Thro' darkest nights its teachings had them cheered,
Prized as the choicest heirloom of their line;
Now yearned they much, that what they thus revered
By secret consolations, long endeared,
Should to their friends and followers hence impart
Its precepts rare; its threat'nings to be feared;
Searching the depths of every human heart,—
Would they had learned it all, as they had learned a part!

X.

But 't is as well; they who behold mankind
Mirrored in ages past, can see that none
Who have reformed the world, but have been blind
To every good in that which they would shun;
And in fell mortal strife, have victories won,
Which they had lost, if less inflamed adverse,
Making the world more pure; but there was ONE,
Reformers heed it when ye seek coerce!—
His charity has purified the Universe!

XI.

Grand sire of Puritàn the tyrant's threat
Defied, when chained he duplicated scrolls;
When King and cringing Parliament had set
Statutes of blood to immolate men's souls.
The creeds of all mankind the King controls,
Aye thoughts and feelings dictates; he, as winds,
Wayward, inconstant; curses;—then extolls;
His own commands, a later hour rescinds,
Reveres the scrolls awhile, then burns like living fiends.

XII.

Must Nations change their faith when kings expire?
Are men parts integrant?　Must they be swayed
By breath of divers monarchs' mere desire?
The mightiest forests bow when winds upbraid;
All bending low on height or slope or glade,
Again erect, to stand, when pass'd the gale:—
Thus strove the tyrant kings to be obeyed;
How gloried stubborn wills to see them fail:—
Nor was the iron hand of power of much avail.

XIII.

Do not the mountain pines that bear the blasts
Of many winters' storms, vast strength attain?
When sweeps the hurricane, its fury casts
To earth whole forests on the extended plain;—
Uprooted, shattered, where its path hath lain;—
But when it smites the storm-trained mountain pines,
Quivering, they stand the swift and fearful strain;
Scarcely a branch dissevered; their long lines
Serried, unbroken, the deep blue of heaven defines.

XIV.

Thus was the will of Puritanic race,
Made as unbending as the mountain pine,
By storms of persecution;—for a space
Alternate with prosperity's sunshine.
A gentle youth, their king, their foes consign
To banishment; their purposes succeed,
Tho' wroth that kingly power would still confine
Their wills within the bounds of his own creed;
They now demand their souls from all decrees be freed.

XV.

Would that the knights, and followers of their faith,
Had been content, while goodly days thus bless;
More fierce than ever, storms of fearful wrath
Follow that respite; mandates merciless,
The wretched peoples fill with dire distress;
That day too passed; men's hopes rose fair again,
Long exiled feet their native shores may press,
Fearless of papal power, but deep their pain
That stern prerogatives dread errors still maintain.

XVI.

Capes, copes, robes, rites, creeds, ceremonies made
To suit the wishes of their enemies;
State policy, wise compromises weighed—
When strong arm'd pow'r, now moulds a faith to please
The shifting-temper of majorities;—
A state religion full of fallacies,
Which all men must believe on pain of death!
Who dares assert it, dictate heresies!
The voice of kings! creatures of mortal breath,—
No, never! Christ is King, sole judge of Christian faith.

XVII.

And all the rights of kings, long held divine,
Were sifted, and the chaff giv'n to the winds;
And men began kings' powers to define,
And show the spirit of self-franchised minds.
Their chivalry, and long submission, blinds—
A wise and kingly Queen maintains strong power—
The many to the issues. But she finds
Dread clouds of conflict o'er the kingdom lower,
And she essays to grasp and crush them in an hour!

XVIII.

She might as well have sought to grasp and crush
The fleecy clouds of heav'n in her weak hands;
'T was vain to smite the air around, to hush
The breezes where the royal palace stands:—
Immortal spirits scorned her proud commands;
True, she might crush the body, but the soul
Was farther from her touch, than o'er the lands,
Lay the fair clouds; far, far 'yond her control;—
Exalted faith extends, despite her care and dole.

XIX.

Aye such a temper Puritàn begot;
He, hungry, sucked it from maternal breasts.
His infancy first lisped it, and he wot
Of popes and bishops, and the sinful tests
Of images, and rites, all that molests
The perfect practice of his father's creed:
The banished clergy knows as welcome guests,
Small hands destroy that which he can not read,
And tiny feet stamp images, nor threat'nings heed.

XX.

His will and conscience strengthen with his strength
He knows what he will have, and he can bear
All that it needeth, to secure at length
Fulfillment of his purpose; tall and fair,
His manly youth betokens tender care;
For much his sire abhorred the frequent sneer
That all his race were rude; his followers there
Untaught and uncouth hinds, their brutish leer
Despised by gentle blood—he felt himself a peer

XXI.

In gaining gentle lore and knowledge deep,
His years were spent, and much he did delight
Chivalrous arms to bear, athletic keep
By exercise untiring, tho' in sight
No badge or token bore, the least to slight
The purest faith, held by his ancestry;
And when he had arrived at manhood's height,
He was aye stalwart, noble, wise was he,
Mingling with courtly knights and dames right worthily.

XXII.

Fearless in Parliament, his voice was heard;
His watchword, Liberty! Altho' the rage
Of princes fell upon him, when the word
Was stifled by thick walls, his pen 'gan wage
A secret war, that nothing could assuage;
When strong armed power prevented labors there,
He fled to other lands, free to engage
In conflicts: learning wisdom every where;
Gaining new strength, for all he deemed the right to dare.

XXIII.

Nor from his early training aught could wean,
Where wise and haughty courtiers seek display
About the sage-accomplished, honored queen:—
Where he as well, now mingled; false array
Sad as deceiving, aye he turned away
More wholly bent to strive for liberty;
For purer faith, more manfully to stay
The subtile purposes of kingly sway;
As years passed on, the many seemed to be
Too hopeless, dull, and blind to their own jeopardy.

XXIV.

Still he despaired not of his native land.
Still gained he followers, he wrote, he spake,
But still the throne and church stood hand in hand;
Tho' their close union he assayed to shake,
Vain was his power, united strength to break;
The suff'rings of his brethren smote his heart,
Dread inquisitions, rack, and sword, and stake,
When faithful followers perish, sore his smart,
Altho' their faith and hope new zeal to men impart.

XXV.

Death promis'd soon relief, for from afar
Another sov'reign comes, free Scotia's hills
Had surely bred a worthy monarch, bar
And ban of sternest subjects' fashioned wills
In many rulers that strong hope instills ;
But he, escaped the hateful bonds that kept
His untamed pride in fetters, quickly fills
Late hopeful Puritàn with grief; he wept;
Unceasing war or exile, which should he accept?

XXVI.

In the fierce fervor of his earlier pride
War had been welcome, and how many now
In his adopted realm, the king defied.
But Puritàn, tho' he did inly vow
To aid his brethren, thro' that dismal slough
Of deep despond, was forced with pain to think
Of turning from the strife, where men allow
Others their own opinions; on the brink
Of sure destruction here, he sole the draught would drink.

8

XXVII.

But there were tender pledges, and he shrank
To have them learn such sorrow, and he knew,
He gone, their life would be a dreary blank;
Thro' tortures, prisons' damps, he felt how few
The years must be, ere death him heavenward drew.
Sore tried to leave the coming conflict, reached
With others, Holland's shores, they there renew
Their broken bonds; thankful their friends beseech'd,
To come to them, where fervently pure faith was preach'd.

XXVIII.

Beloved was Puritàn,—respected, prized:
This, his adopted land, revered him, when
Agents of wrath his king had authorized
To seize him, and return to thralldom then,
That he might soon decay in noisome pen;
But it is writ elsewhere, how for the good
Of future generations he 'gan ken
New England's savage shores—how brave he stood
Firm on that frozen coast, 'twixt wave and wood:
Thanking his God for far and peaceful solitude.

XXIX.

And of his brethren in the realm what fate?
Save those that later joined the infant State,
Proud, bigoted, more selfish, they intent
To hold their homes their high ambition sate,
Blindly contend—fight on, nor once relent
Until the realm is in a wild ferment;
Success attends them, theirs at length the power;

No Kings, no Bishops, long, long hoped-for hour—
Attained thro' seas of blood! but discontent
Follows usurped, unhallowed government—
Glad to escape the storms that threat'ning lower,
King—priests restore—for refuge fly to Puritàn's far tower!

PURITAN.

CANTO THE FIFTH.

THE SETTLEMENT.

I.

WHO is the noblest? He who proud and strong,
Advances on the tide of life, to sway
The sword or sceptre o'er the excited throng,
Wars for the right, and vanquishes the wrong,
Glorying if need be, casts his life away
Valiant and fervent in the foremost fray,
Fame him alluring, while hot passion gives
A reckless, headlong, eagerness alway,
That untold wonders in its course achieves
Renown from praiseful hosts, for deeds in arms receives?

II.

Or is he most heroic, who can bear
With patience, pangs that none but God can see,
Making the good of others his sole care,
Sore laboring day by day, tho' there can be
No present fruits; striving on cheerfully,
Bearing and suffering, faithful; when decay
His earthly hopes, gaining humility?
Hail! moral hero! heavenly chivalry!
As far as souls outvalue mortal clay,
This, that,—and only these their heavenly Guide obey.

(57)

III.

The mighty ship lay safe, but from the shore
Twelve weary furlongs; every day with pain,
Waiting the rising tide, with travail sore,
Great Puritàn to man the bark was fain,
Striving with oar and sail the land to gain;
There in the wet cold blasts, they timber fell,
Exposed to blinding snows and sleet and rain,
And hew and heave, seek mortar, thatch as well,
Each night o'er stormy waves regain their citadel.

IV.

Oh! what long, weary, toilsome, sorrowing moons,
To those who watched their labor on the land
The stormy nights, or gained the wretched boons,
To slumber on the ship, where suffering band
Pine in the fœtid air; they pallid stand,
Praying them haste, e'en rudest shelter rear,
For much, alas! their needs such change demand;
Alarmed, they knew the savage hordes too near,
Their forms, and rising smoke, on every side appear.

V.

As ever-toiling Puritàn returned
From labor for their homes, or from pained quests
Of ever-hiding savages, he yearn'd
Remove the ills, his followers distressed;
Sick'ning and dying friends his soul oppress'd,
Death from his followers' arms, their dearest tore,
Sad mothers cast their young, strong sires contest
The fatal darts, but soon their comrades bore
Them dead, and added these, to those they'd wept before

VI.

'To grief for them, was added keener woe;
'The tender offspring of his love had borne
'The Ocean blasts; but keener winds did blow
From circling frozen coasts; blithesome at morn,
At night he came, the mother trembling, worn,
Held to her anguished breast her suffering child;
At dawn, the icy form the sire had torn,
With silent sorrow, from her pressure wild,
Teaching the lowliest there, to be so reconciled.

VII.

His darling languished; nearest, dearest one,
Pine not so sorely on this dreary day!
How much they need him! here and there nigh lone,
He tends the languid couch; so many lay
Diseased—scarce half a score to help allay
Their suff'rings; these him aid; they bear the dead,
They keep the stealthy savages at bay;
Oh! fearful days! oh nights of drearihead!
The weeks seemed years, and yet too soon they sped.

VIII.

Each time, when constant pressing care, permits
Him cheer his frail, and now more fragile fair,
Striving impart love's potent benefits,
He grieved to mark her silver-threaded hair;
Tho' his each fond endeavor of wise care,
How faint and pallid, clear each ebbing vein!
Vain prayer for life, but not God's will to bear,
Afar from her lost darling, she is lain
In that long row 'neath frozen sod, along the main.

IX.

Thus weariest portion of the toil is his!
Thus fails no pang of deepest drearihead!
To weep her dead, his children motherless!
Ah me! ah me! she was too daint'ly bred,
Too tenderly, too frail, when here bestead
Such weathers, and such sorrow; little babe!
Her heart could not keep warm, when thou wert dead;
She laid her life away as 't were a trabe,
The child, her darling, was her spirit-astrolabe.

X.

Why tell it? only He who knows the heart,
Knows what they suffered, for their every moan
Was stifled, lest it knowledge should impart
Of their increasing weakness; never a groan,
As they buried in grief the dearest one;
The savages so nigh, so watchful too;
The graves were levelled, thick with seed were sown,
For at the first, they were alas! too few
To help brave Puritàn rear homes, and foes subdue!

XI.

But when the warm winds blew, and birds 'gan sing,
The sinking were refreshed; and soon came days
Of sunny warmth.   Welcome! ye buds of spring!
Winter is past; their burden'd hearts always
In deep thanksgiving, they rejoice to raise!
Now from the forest comes bold *Samoset;*
"Welcome!" upon his lips, a welcome phrase,
In that dear speech of England! never yet,
Tho' feigning diffidence, did word more hope beget!

XII.

The big ship weighed her anchors, and her prow
Turned for old England. Calm was Puritàn,
Yet, touched by grief for others, bade them now
Return, if any mourned his earlier vow;
No, never! child, nor maid, nor wife, nor man!
True was this tried, and ever faithful van!
Tho' half of them had died, their trust in Him
Whom they had vow'd to serve, life's narrow span
Was undiminished; when earth's hopes grew dim,
Faith entered heav'n, joining the joys of Seraphim.

XIII.

The last link was dissevered, from their ken
Slow swaying, moved the ship! how swell'd the heart,
Yearning in vain for pow'r of utt'rance then!
Striving its wild emotions to impart,
Yet silent, thro' some sad mysterious art;
Still Puritàn forbade the sacrifice!
"Yon ship sole voice 'twixt whom these waters part;
Ye sorely tried! I feel what yearnings rise!
Go! 'tis your native land, tho' princes tyrannize."

XIV.

There rose no vagrant impulse; they had done
All things devoutly, and deep grief can bind
The heart like joy: that earth from them had won,
Pledges to bind them to it, had the mind
Not otherwise for dwelling been inclined;
So stood they firm, tho' weeping, as the sails
Filled from the West; obedient to the wind
She parted the dark waters; slowly trails
The helm; the troubled sea, the narrow coast bewails!

9

XV.

Long strained each eye, until the less'ning mass
Faded in depths of azure; naught was there
Betwixt the sea and sky; yet glances pass,
Gladsome and wondering, when upon the ear
Falls the slow pulsing air, and they can hear
The last low volley in a long farewell!
Still restless waves along the shore appear,
Some tidings of that voyaging to tell;
But nights and days that last fond trace dispell'd as well.

XVI.

Through all the summer long were cheerful days;
The corn was gladsome green, and fruits began
To ripen from the blossoms; many ways
Thro' the deep forest, or where tangled ran
O'er thickets teeming vines, forbidding man
Trespass the shadowy haunts, were beauties rare;
The sea, the sky, the land, divinest plan
With ever varying details; flowers fair,
Insects and birds, 'mid leaves and fruits commingled there.

XVII.

Berries grew on the bushes 'mid the grass;
Sweet plums and cherries and the amber grapes.
There wealth of fishes might belief surpass;
No goodly gift denied them, when escapes
Their golden harvest from the phantom shapes
Of frosts and blightings, and is safely stored:—
Vast flocks of fowls enter the circling capes;
Unhoped-for wealth of luxuries! Each board
Groans with the feast; their God in thanks and praise adored.

XVIII.

The joys and sorrows of those faithful few,
Why tell? fast friends, aye peers of Puritàn—
Worthy, as honored; humble, yet how true;
But Puritàn's high purpose far outran
Their simple hopes, their slow expanding plan;
He saw their little village but a dot
Upon a vasty shore; enrapt would scan
The sailless ocean, or would seek some spot
To gaze to West, o'er lands whose breadth no mortal wot.

XIX.

Yet ceased he not from labor for their good;
Spared much, for heav'n had giv'n them this abode;
Fierce habitants had once this solitude
Denied, now perished utterly.   He strode
Thro' all their haunts, and saw how death had mowed
The native race, like weeds, as 'twere to plant
The better peoples, God had there bestowed;
But other tribes anear were arrogant,
Saving great Massasoit, he, true as adamant.

XX.

Once when the Indian monarch fell disease
Had smitten unto death—the fearless knight
Hastened alone, daring all jeopardies,
Thro' pathless forests traced his way aright,
Spared by each wondering savage, till in sight
Of death-doomed chieftain's dwelling; there he found
How wailing wives and pow wows, sad unite
Their tears with thronging subjects, to confound
And conjure forth grim death, with groans that might astound.

XXI.

It was a new but grateful task, and straight,
Not resting from his travel, Puritàn
Sought how he might his pangs alleviate,
His parching fever to assuage began;
His dark and swollen tongue, he, speechless, wan,
Relaxed its rigor; soon such tender care
Bro't back his life; they praised the Godlike man,
For wondrous potent power, that could repair
The ravages of death, and fond allegiance swear!

XXII.

" Know, mighty chieftain," said that grateful prince,
" What dangers here enthrong you—Corbatant
Obbatin—Canacum—sachem and pinse
Bound in fierce wrath, and solemn covenant,
To smite the strangers who their lands would plant;
Theirs, all *their* past—theirs, where in wild excess
The beasts and fowls and fishes, none shall daunt
With strange report of arms, whose mightiness
Can pierce the dark and far off ear with pangs distress.

XXIII.

" Sure as yon sun shall sink beneath the West
So sure such foe will smite; they only seek
A fitting moment when unguarded rest
Shall make more sure their vengeance; fearful, weak,
But for an hour, they watchful, quick will wreak
Such fury on you, that no living soul
Shall 'scape to tell the tale, or aid bespeak;—
Strike then, the first—appalled in utmost dole,
Their chieftains gone, the warriors you may eath control."

XXIV.

" Never," said Puritàn, "never will I
Strike the first blow on these defenseless hordes;
' *Seeking the calm repose of Liberty* '
I came in peace, and peaceful will aby,
So long as these give ear to peaceful words;
But I am wary, and these unsheathed swords,
Are sharp, two edg'd, and glitt'ring as yon sun;
Let them but shoot an arrow, and the cords
Of this fond faith dissever! I will shun
No direful deed of blood, until they are undone."

XXV.

"It is as well, Oh hero! for I see
Portents by divination; these have been
Thro' many generations, fierce and free,—
Untrammell'd as untutor'd, now to ween
O'erwhelming power, swift, fatal, tho' unseen,
A baneful presence and in vain assailed;
Aye it is galling,—savage hate how keen!
What seas of blood will flow, ere are unveiled
The mighty lands to West, fate vainly countervai.ed!

XXVI.

" Fate known in vain; death drew the vei., and clear
Flitted the sure perspective; as the day
Dawns in the East, as earliest gleams appear,
The stars evanish; fade they—fade away!
The Sun spares not the rarest galaxy!
Ye! children of the Sun! your day just dawns;
We fill the land, as stars the night array;
As grows your strength, our joy forever wans;
Yet in your triumph fear,—fear most the foe that fawns.

XXVII.

"The stars of heaven fade calmly from the sight;
Not so will these; as meteors expire,
As pass the comets, waking wild affright,
As dart the lightnings with consuming fire,
In midday wreaking wide, destruction dire,
So will these war!   Thus ruthlessly decay,
Yet none the less they perish, and their ire
Undying, self-consuming, speeds the day
Free in the blest abodes 'neath Kictan's sway;
Free, for in life or death they must be free alway.

XXVIII.

"But fear *me* not; have I not made my vow?
When was my truth dishonored; me and mine
To thee and thine will be true friends; but now,
My life was in thy hands, thy power divine
Was fond to frustrate e'en death's dark design;
Thou seest the leafless trees in yonder wood;—
Stalwart and distant, tho' the twigs entwine;
So dwell the native tribes, strong, unsubdued,
Scant peopling vast, far-stretching lands, else solitude.

XXIX.

"But races thine will throng the mighty land!
As multitudinous as in the days
Of coming summer, will the leaves expand
Upon the forest trees; see how decays
The forest! mark the fields! see how they raise
Cities and villages!   There structures rise
Like hills, like mountains, see! what wondrous ways
On sea and lake, and river,—they entice
Those mighty floats! farewell! my native Paradise!"

XXX.

It filled the knight with rapture, for he oft
Had had strange visions, and succeeding dreams
Of wondrous exaltation ; he aloft
Was wont to seek for succor, and he deems
Heaven lights his soul with these celestial beams,
T' impart fresh strength and fervor ; strong he treads
A homeward path ; his brain with projects teems
To haste such consummation ; fancy spreads
Fair villages about him, nor dread labor dreads.

XXXI.

Time passed, and his few followers felt repose ;
Sweet respite from long labors, strong and wise,
They had secured the end for which they chose
To dare the Ocean's unknown jeopardies.
Their pray'rs and thanks, unquestion'd, heav'nward rise ;
But not so eath content was Puritàn ;—
In near adventure or far enterprise
To quell oft-rising dangers, or to scan
The land and shores about them—hope thro' ages ran.

XXXII.

Full many a site he chose, and chiefly one
Near, to his soul enticing, thro' the bay
Studded with countless islands, he had gone
To greet the sachem queen, beyond where lay
The wanton colony, whose soon decay
Left ruin'd Wessagusset, those, (men tell)
Had Puritàn defended valiantly,
From sure destruction ; he supreme to quell
The riotous strangers, and the savage hordes as well.

XXXIII.

His emprize thus accomplished, yearned his heart
To seek the far-off turmoiled hopeless scene
Of freedom's struggles in the realm, t' impart
True knowledge of the lands his eye had seen—
The heritage of freedom—he had been
Long years to man securing; o'er the sea,
The frequent ships bro't tidings he did ween,
Pregnant with undream'd horrors, this must be
A refuge for his brethren from all tyranny!

XXXIV.

The fort was finished; and its bristling ports
Looked watchful, o'er the village and the bay;
Their favor now, each wily sachem courts;
True friends to guard new sites, lest foes betray—
He secretly set sail, vast schemes to lay
Before his kindred in his native land.
What hosts shall rise his power to obey!
The sea shall groan, as countless sails expand,
To waft to West, the untold hosts of his command.

PURITAN.

CANTO THE SIXTH.

LABORS IN ENGLAND.

I.

" PAUSE! Ye who hold the fate of nations, pause!
    Ye stand upon destruction's brink, nor weet
The ruin that awaits you; leave the cause
For fools to prate of, and prepare to meet
Events fast consummating, or defeat
Sudden, o'erwhelming, fairest hopes will blight
Ye never can restore; what foul deceit
And selfishness perverts all sense of right!
Ponder each issue! Choose and act with wise foresight.

II.

" Ye stand, as stood the host of Israel,
Enthronging low the valley, from whose ken
The gathering storm was hid, until it fell
In overwhelming fury; I, as when—
Elijah stood on Carmel—prayed he then—
His watchman marked the cloud, small as a hand,
Rise from the sea, quick warning thoughtless men—
As Ahab hastened on at his command,
Spar'd from the rains and blasts that drench'd the thirsty
        land.

10   (69)

III.

" Hasten to flee the wrath that waits you here,
Laud, Strafford, and false Finch, without remorse,
Make freemen fettered slaves; each horrid fear
Of past accursed reign, with twofold force
Is growing into fact; from hellish source,
The double stream of kings and priestly sway,
Is stirring wrath in its resistless course,
Now big with ruin; tho' the flood ye stay,
Such triumph as defeat the nation will dismay.

IV.

" Why hesitate, oh! weak and selfish men!
Are not the bravest, the most daring there?
Sure as the earth's foundations—there and then
Was laid the corner stone of structure rare,
That ye shall help build up, if ye do bear
Yourselves as worthy such a weighty charge:
For Solomon, King David did prepare
Exhaustless riches, that he might enlarge
God's glory; well ye wot he did his part discharge,

V.

"And reared a temple of undream'd-of art;
Cedar from Lebanon, and algum trees,
O'erlaid with gold composed each holiest part;
Rich gold of Parvaim, fine filagrees
Of beaten gold, and carvèd ivories,
And precious stones, unnumbered; strangers wrought
In silver, iron, brass; across far seas,
Thousands of skillful workmen wisely sought.
Conception grand;—thus wisely to completion brought.

VI.

" Your fathers have amass'd the wealth ye need
Of spiritual riches; thousands stand
Waiting to give wise aid, in word and deed,
Ready to give strong aid, with heart and hand;
Be ye but faithful to your Lord's command,
And skillful laborers will the work advance
With zeal untiring, till th' inviting land
Shall groan beneath the structure; heaven's expanse
Grow brighter o'er that Temple's domed magnificence.

VII.

" The wondrous vision unto me was brought
The middle watch of night, when deepest sleep
Falleth on man; fear came upon me, fraught
With trembling, which made all my flesh to creep,
The very hairs thereof stood up, and deep,
Deep awe made all my timorous bones to shake.
Instant the spirit seemed thro' space to sweep—
Forms vast confused beheld—a voice loud spake,
'The task is thine,' ah sure my soul was well awake.

VIII.

" The holy vision, perfect faith esteems;—
As I have dwelt upon that fruitful shore,
As I have learned the wealth with which it teems,
As I have heard, as I have seen far more,
As He hath given me light whom I adore;
Upon the finished summit, I have stood,
High o'er the earth, exalted, to explore
The untold realm; 'mid heaven's solitude,
The varied land, vision prophetic clearly viewed—

IX.

" Two Oceans clasped the continent, where moored
Navies on either shore; all nations seemed
To bring rich commerce, and each vale allured
Thy multitud'nous offspring; cities teemed
With countless hosts, each stream with wealth undreamed ;
Nor think to sail from sea to sea, thro' space
Narrow united—mountain heights far gleamed,
Wide severed by vast valleys, brightly trace,
Vast rivers there, how far they flow, whence springs en-
    lace!

X

" High from the airy Temple's sunny dome,
I gazed entranced; and mark'd the peoples there,
Like summer bees, as ladened thick they come
About the busy hive; with earnest cheer,
Enthronging dense laborious every where :
What cities, towns and villages, what homes,
Dotting the cultured fields; how peaceful fair !
What tho' the storm in dark'ning fury comes,
It passes, and the land its busy life resumes.

XI.

" More glorious than Coliseum vast,
The eternal edifice from whence I gazed ;
The circling columns human art surpassed ;
Like sunbeams of the moted air, they raised
Story on story, while the eye amazed
Stretched thro' the soft perspective, far away—
Till 'neath Auroras, thro' the air unhazed
Where gleaming ices caught each starry ray ;
So far, its glist'ning collonades to northward lay.—

XII.

" Nor failed they in the tropics, where the skies
Were deep and cloudless; lofty palm-trees waved
Beneath the airy arches, where the rise
Of circling shores most gorgeous blooms engraved.
And yet, to where the Oceans softly laved
The unworn columns, with their constant flow;
How far the shores the golden pavements paved!
About me gathered folds, whose crimson glow
Contrasted with the cloud-like lines of dazzling snow.—

XIII.

"And high, aloft, the countless stars of light
Gleamed on the azure; fell a shadiness
Sudden and flitting; mark'd I near in sight,
The strong-winged Eagle, the empyrean press,
Slow swaying to the West, with haughtiness;
His eye, undaunted, fixed upon the sun,
Fresh as tho' yesterday in Rome's distress
He had disdained abide; her shame to shun—
Imperial power lost, Westward had Empire won.

XIV.

" Now caught the ear far pæans of liberty!
Freedom forever! thro' united power!
From frigid North the strains intensify;
From farthest West, where mighty mountains tower;
From farthest East, augmenting every hour;
Thunders of ' Liberty and Union, now,
Forever! one, inseparable !' 'gan lower
Dread storms, but peals swept on, to where palms bow
In solemn murmurs, echoing back the nation's vow."

XV.

Thus spake the hero; and the list'ning throng,
Intent and wondering, raised the loud acclaim
Of "Liberty!" "New England!" cheers prolong,
Until the prudent knight, in middest came
With warnings, lest too boisterous zeal inflame,
Their adversaries' hearts.   In councils sage,
His friends and followers meeting, faith proclaim,
Ever in secret, lest such zeal enrage
The stubborn powers that hold e'en souls in vassalage.

XVI.

Sped he thro'out the West;—peasant and peer
Listened whenever power, argus-eyed,
Seemed wanting vigilance.   Some, scorning fear,
Attended midnight prayer, or hushed would glide
At eve or dawn, to where he prophesied;
From far and wide, soul-stirring Puritàn
Gathered conventicles of sorely-tried,
Men, just and brave: speeding the godly plan
Of truth, of liberty, full franchisement of man.

XVII.

"Seek not effect such purpose," once he cried,
"In this polluted realm, wailing thro' time;
True, we have kept alive, else had it died,
The flame of Liberty; oh! how sublime,
Could it but blaze, high as yon heaven climb!
But what a spark, how dim, it scarcely glows;
To fan its flickering flame is held a crime!
Why wear your lives away in fruitless throes?
There an uncumber'd continent high heaven bestows.

XVIII.

"Haste to possess it; native monarchs there
Across yon Ocean beckon you to come;
Kindly and faithful, they have promised share
The exhaustless lands o'er which they idly roam;
Or prove they false, and sudden wrath assume
What are they, naked, with their puny arms?
As leaves before the winds, or Ocean's foam
Before the gale evanishing—their harms—
One blast of missiles ours, a mighty host alarms."

XIX.

He, eloquent, convinced with stirring words;
But when the thoughtless, or the wanton press'd
To eager haste, hot-headed, brandish'd swords,
With ribald oaths, and fickle souls confessed,
"Stay! stay!" he cried, "it needeth not attest
True zeal with blasphemy; this work requires
Sore labor, righteousness, it needs the best,
Of steady fearless purpose, calm desires,
Strong trust in God, true faith, patience that never tires.

XX.

"But shrink not, oh! ye worthy! from the pains;
Whatever was accomplished from the first
Without sore travail? He who long refrains
In pride or sloth from labor, is accurs'd;
The fallacies of ease, too fondly nursed,
By pampered luxury's minions in this land,
Wake vengeance; suffering, hunger, cold, and thirst
The least—the times strong energies demand;
Pure hearts, clear minds, strong arms in righteousness to stand.

XXI.

" Brave to advance the dignity of toil,
The worth of labor, as a means and end;
Not solely to secure ignoble spoil,
Of worldly riches,—but the blood to send
Throbbing, and healthful; know ye, souls depend
Upon this vital action; and the mind
Uninjured by disease, is free to spend
It vigor in achievement; souls to find
Food for development for heaven, as God designed.

XXII.

" Far in the East, the myriad slaves exist,
To toil forever at a monarch's will;
To rear vast monuments, that may resist
All change for ages; monuments of skill,
Eternal monuments, that well may fill
Posterity with wonder; tasks like those
Prove Power absolute, pregnant with ill;
Fearful discrepancy, one will to impose
What million hands must execute without repose.

XXIII.

" Where are the haunts, where are the homes of these?
Of individuality, there lives
No trace, save these, of their past miseries:—
In nearer past, enlightened power strives
Create thro' zeal, enlightened donatives,
T' advance its selfish ends; where beauteous art,
Exquisitely wrought matter still survives,
Expressive of the exalted soul, true heart,
Know liberty alone can genius life impart.

XXIV.

"A noble and enlighten'd kingly sway,
Gives freedom to each individual soul;
Unshadowed by dread Upas' power, art may
Freely spring up and blossom, for control
Imagination brooks not; and in dole
The intellectual suffers, to express
Its knowledge; virtue, would the world console;
　Wise power will be an atmosphere to bless
Such rare fruition,—tho' its end is selfishness.

XXV.

"But why to thee these thoughts of kingdoms tell?
Ye would away with empire, as the vast
But too unwieldy Roman empire fell
Into decay, ye would that men should cast
All kingdoms into atoms.　Ye may blast
Your own best hopes with rashness; men must learn
Wise lessons of self-knowledge; speaks the past,
　They must be wise who would be free; must yearn
With toil for knowledge, that the right they may discern.

XXVI.

"Strangely the Course of Empire Westward moves!
And when, to reach a new world's shore, it needs
O'er yon vast Ocean float, it well behooves
Him who a nation's founders thither leads,
Deeply to ponder, as his toil proceeds.
Spain sought with untold wealth and pow'r to build
An empire on that continent; what deeds,
　What toils heroic there, by brave, proud-willed,
Strong armed, undaunted knights, with burning ardor fill'd!

I I

XXVII.

" Did not Columbus toil, and plead, and pray?
Did not heroic Cortez labor there,
Performing deeds of valor, many a day,
Toils which great Hercules had shrunk to bear?
Did not Balboa strive with anxious care,
Far o'er the steep vast Andes, to transport
Piecemeal great ships, did he to labor spare?
And yet Pizarro, he did travail court,
Sore toils on land and sea, for ends of basest sort?

XXVIII.

"Such efforts for the most, secured success;
But came an end of Conquest, and the gold
E'en of Peru, and Mexico still less,
The fine wrought gold was gone; what wealth untold
The mountain mines still from their grasp might hold,
None knew; but it must be secured by toil
Of human hands—the means which must unfold
All earth's resources—these, their hands ne'er soil,
Should Spain's Grandees there dig and delve, tho' gold the
      spoil!

XXIX.

" They could to death work slaves, fight who might there
Develop what they could not; but their land
A century long, hath lain forlorn and bare,
Accursed by proud idolatrous command;
Long as their rule so let it barren stand;
Nor bring forth gold to crush with haughty pow'r,
The infancy of nations, that demand
To labor for their rights, now comes the hour
For *their* deserved supremacy; tyrants must cow'r.

XXX.

" Haste—haste ye, to possess the inviting shore!
Make labor there a duty and a pride;
Laugh him to scorn who scorns, and more and more
Prove to the world, the blessings that abide
With those who God obey; toiling, confide
To Him there labour's issue; he who sows
Shall reap; not selfishly—for thus allied
Allegiance to the State secures repose,
And all will vie t'support its laws and smite its foes.

XXXI.

" He will make the wilderness like Eden;
Thanksgiving, and the voice of melody,
Peace, joy, and gladness, will be found therein;
Come, come ye warm brave hearts, yours shall it be
To give rich blessings to posterity!
—Tho' ye may suffer, and must labor sore—
God's truth, and righteousness, and liberty,
'There shall a man be precious'—yea, far more—
More precious than fine-beaten gold in goodly store.

XXXII.

" Each one shall help his neighbor; there shall be
No lords, no class proscribed, each man shall strive
Helpful to be to each;—right speedily
The work shall prosper, not a soulless hive,
Where rulers by the toils of thousands thrive,
Vast monuments of grandeur to uprear;
No tokens of such bonds will there revive,
But on the plains, and o'er the hills appear,
Dear homes, to each the best reward, evermore dear.

XXXIII.

"Each from his cottage door shall see the green
Of God's own fields, the shrubs, the many trees,
In fullest leaf; and pluck the fruits I ween;
And each shall hear the waters' melodies
Murmuring concert with the harmonies
Of birds, and breathe the pure fresh air of heaven;
And see the clouds changed by each shifting breeze,
And yon great azure dome, at starry ev'n,
At noon, at dawn; a sight these mists have seldom given.

XXXIV.

" There free and pure may little children play,
And aged parents rest them from their cares;
For competence and comfort will repay
Wise toil, frugality and fervor theirs;
Old age, of health, and happiness and prayers,
A blessing gives remote posterity,
The soul for entrance into heaven prepares.
Will ye not choose such life, has luxury
Or ease a single hope, of such prosperity?"

PURITAN.

FINAL SUCCESS.

I.

NOT unsuccessful, was the fervent zeal
    Of Puritàn; it won the sure reward
Such toil must ever win.   God did reveal
To him, hate, pride, and avarice to ward,
Conflicting interests to make accord;
And tho' the king had set his seal to give
That Continent away—accounted Lord
Of what he had not won—prerogative
How vain!   Was not the land for those who there should live?

II.

He mingled in the thickest of the fray;
Sandys, Virginius' friend, espoused his cause,
Coke, powerfully pleading, swept away
The fallacies of Kings' unrighteous laws;
Vainly the council to its measures draws
The strong defense of Avalon's pure zeal,
The energy of Gorges, kings applause;
In parliament the wisest ill conceal
The deep concern for Puritàn's success all feel.

(81)

III.

For Lord-Proprietors, would sit at ease
Within the realm, and hands must hasten thence
To labor, and return their gains to these;
Aye it was futile; well the world might stare,
When they in wrath command a knight repair
To that far coast, equipped to hold the land
Far stretching, and the restless sea; nor spare
Who dared his net to spread along the strand,
Or on the mighty shores, untaxed, presume to stand.

IV.

Mason and Gorges merit praise, not scorn;
They helped the mighty work, not as they wished,
But as He willed; their day was passed; the morn
Of brighter day was dawning; those assist
Who thought its coming they might eath resist;
Sir Alexander, armed him at their call,
From far-off Scotia (of the gift ye wist)
To fight their battles; he was brave and tall,
He reached their coast, he sailed along, and that was all.

V.

Saving a name for Scotland, all his toil
Was fruitless; won he not a rood of land
Upon the continent; 't was wished-for spoil,
Yet when he saw the countless bays expand,
The wild, cold rocky coast his care demand,
Dark on the deep dark waters, and the gloom,
Deep dark as Ocean, where the forests stand,
He turned away disheartened, to assume
Power there, against the power of France who would pre-
        sume?

VI.

With singleness of purpose, naught could daunt,
Pressed Puritàn his suit; with knights allied,
The best, and bravest, entered Troynovant;
Now gave new hopes, new fervor, friends supplied
Gold in profusion; tho' the court decried
From all contending claimants, he secured
The land washed by two Oceans, for so wide
The vision told—nor less had he endured—
Vague limits, but the hopes were clear which them allured.

VII.

Lest foes might breed dissensions, turned he hence;
A doughty knight, and one he trusted well,
Straight he dispatched to prove the land's defense,
While he within the realms might still compel
Fast friends to hasten thither; seeking quell
The rising humors of his enemies.
Brave Endicot, to that far citadel,
Despite the raging Ocean's jeopardies,
Thy faithful spouse, thy babes thou bearest as sureties,

VIII.

Of faith, of zeal sincere, of sure success!
And with what earnest cheer upon that shore
So far and wild, Conant's long loneliness—
Watching since Puritàn's long leave before—
Was ended; friends rejoicing more and more,
When they had learned these faithful knights there dwelt
With full an hundred followers, with store
Of all things needful; kindly He had dealt
With those who had advanced His cause, true fervor felt.

IX.

Still spread the Godly leaven, far and near,
Earnest, courageous followers, rose and armed
To conquer in His service; joy sincere,
Glowing imaginations, wak'ning charmed
The doubting; not the weakest were alarmed,
By Ocean's dangers, or the wild shore's gloom;
These were not exiles that rude power had harmed,
They were the cheerful followers, glad to assume
For Him e'en poverty, and care, nor feared the tomb.

X.

If there was more chivalric fire, the day
The hermit Peter roused the faithful hosts
Thro' all the West, to arm, and make their way
For far-off Palestine's untraveled coasts,
To win the Holy Tomb from baleful hosts
Of hated infidels—here was true zeal,
Intense, enduring;   fervently it boasts
A nobler purpose, for the whole world's weal,
To win a realm for Christ, and His pure truth reveal.

XI.

To yon poor heathens perishing for light;
His chosen servants welcome weal or woe;
Enraptured scores attend the Godly knight;
The crowded ships the waves wash to and fro,
Deep sinking in the waters, forth they go,
In valiant chaplain's and brave knight's command;
For Puritàn yet lingers to bestow
Blessing he must with vital strength demand,
Lest hostile powers within the realm his hopes withstand.

XII.

For he had felt the bonds that so enthralled
Virginius in his labors, and to look
For justice from far councils sore appalled
His anxious heart; far-seeing faith could brook
The monarch's insincerity, but shook
To think how foes, aye, friends, might harm his cause,
Or future powers molest their chosen nook
Far off and unprotected; crush with laws
Which he could not prevent; he wished not man's applause,

XIII.

Still less, to be dependent on the will
Of any human; 'twixt him and his God,
No creature to impose e'en rules that fill
His soul with fervor; he toward heaven would plod
His chosen way alone, if others trod
Obedient to the word, and inner light,
He had discerned, submissive to his nod,
These he rejoiced to welcome, and aright
Champions of freedom and free faith attend the knight.

XIV.

Soon others blindly, or for selfish ends
Yielding to his persuasion, gave command,
And well-nigh every power to his true friends;
'Twas wisely done, a powerful, bold band,
Unflinching, zealous, wise, united stand;
And warily, th' ambiguous clauses writ
Transfer, the few perceive it, to his hand,
The rule of that far planting; benefit,
Beyond all words, sage hero for that work how fit!

I 2

XV

If there was zeal before, now ardor burned ;
Enthusiasm warmed the nation's heart ;
Hundreds flocked to his standards, and there turned
A fleet with anxious prows, chafing to start ;
Knights and fair women fervently impart
Strength, purity ; and children seemed inspired
To lend their aid, with fond and simple art ;
Teachers, prophetically wise, conspired
To speed the mighty work with faith and strength untired

XVI.

The body-corporate launched on the sea !
The rudimental state, seeking abode,
Bearing its subtly-chartered liberty ;
Subjects and rulers, variously bestowed
On many ships, the stormy waters rode ;
How many hundreds followed where he led !
How many pure and godly hearts there glowed
With speechless fervor ! as they onward sped.
Disease and danger tried their hearts, yet none misled.

XVII.

As when the sun, advancing from the East,
Brightens the far horizon, glowing hues
Of brilliancy, by nearing beams increased,
Until the clouds, effulgent light imbues,
Each moment deepening, till the gazer rues
The blinding glories of the full-orbed sun ;
Then earth, the rays receives in sparkling dews,
Infinite hues of beauty she has won ;
Dark clouds, late fair, those rays enfold and earth has none

XVIII.

But earth is little saddened, light is fair,
  The zenith blue, the fields a fresh glad green,
And e'en the dismal clouds embosom there
  The glowing sunshine, tho' it may be seen
But heavenward, above thro' space serene;
So seemed the valiant hosts, that Puritàn
  Now led afar; imaginations sheen
Had lit the far horizon, and outran
Dull reason—then their brightest tinted hopes began.

XIX.

They beamed upon them, every thing aglow;
  Their plans perfected, on the sea they ride;
But clouds o'er shadow dark, as on they go,
  Disease, sore sorrows—how their souls were tried
Yet found they life and light, the heavenward side.
Upon the lonely undeveloped shore,
  None felt repining—faithfully they bide
His will, heaven seemed more near, low bending o'er
These devotees, than where hosts worship'd Him before.

XX.

To bear not grudgingly, but with a soul
  Cheerful, submissive to the Father's will!
Blest christian principle, that shall control
  The Universe; the purposes fulfill
Of Him who died to stem earth's flood of ill;
Kingdom of heaven on earth—Thy will be done;
  Humility, forgiveness, love instill;
For thus God's tender grace is surely won;
With all the power of God, He was the lowliest one,

XXI.

This is an area where all may strive;
Who is the lowliest, the rudest born—
Who is the loftiest of all alive—
Station is nothing, may ye not all mourn,
And bear disease, or pain, reproach, or scorn?
Ye all may suffer, aye—ye shall, and must;
But never grief like His hath any borne;
It is God's roll of honor; He is just;
The least shall be the greatest: sorrowing ones, have trust.

XXII.

Life, health, friends, ease and goodly nourishment,
Riches and luxuries, men strive to gain;
But Puritàn's brave hosts there underwent
The loss of every thing, that men are fain
To prize.   What numbers died! they suffered pain,
And famine, toil, and grief on barren coast,
A strip betwixt terrific stormy main,
And forests dense, primeval. where a host
Of treach'rous natives made their evil deeds their boast,

XXIII.

To win free space to pray!—it was indeed
A very Bethel; tho' he never saw
The angels that descended, thence to lead
Their lost ones up to heaven, sure he did draw
Deep inspirations from God's love and law.
Had Charitè survived—Humilitè
In love been won, that sad self-righteous flaw
His noble heart had grieved. Intolera
Alas! inflamed each fault. tainting posterity.

XXIV.

There formed they embryonic villages,
Along the Ocean, where the ships might ride;
Of their past lands and lives sole vestiges;
Ye ships! ye are a blessing and a pride!
Ye ministering spirits of the wide,
Wide earth, and Ocean-severed continents.
Without your aid, the waters that divide
The lands, had ever been admonishments
Of impotence, as are the subtler elements.

XXV.

Are ye not voices? sure from shore to shore
Ye breathe fond words, and speak from mind to mind,
Words of deep knowledge, power, inspired lore!
And ye are hands, to bear to all mankind
Most precious gifts; ah! human hearts ye bind
In love, far peoples send their treasures where
Ye tell who needeth, and the favoring wind,
The breath of God, doth onward deign to bear
Your white wings full against the blue so wondrous fair.

XXVI.

Would they could lift you from the dark abyss,
And bear you upward thro' the deep'ning blue!
When, when will man attain that yearned-for bliss?
The lark rebukes his ignorance, it knew
Ages ago to soar; the eagle flew
With mighty wings, its wisdom from the first!
Man's growing knowledge could the sea subdue,
Light, heat, he made to serve him; lightning durst
To tame; but gravitation's bonds, when will he burst?

XXVII.

Oh ships! strong wing'd, swift, faithful agencies,
Taught by the mind of man ye have built up
This continent! the deathless energies
Of wise Colono, dared with thee to grope
Beyond the limits of all other's hope:
Ye led the boldest to possess this land,
Brought builders, all things needful, strong to cope
With every ill: ye decked the barren strand,
And made the Seas as highways as men's needs demand.

XXVIII.

Here was the spirit dear to Puritàn;
Men eager for achievement; wise to advance
The welfare of the State; it straight began
To prosper; ships sped o'er the wide expanse,
Intent with fostering care, its weal t' enhance.
The peoples, fearless, full of enterprise,
Pressed onward for abode or sustenance;
Or by adventurous spirits led, surprise
The far-off forests, and new regions civilize.

XXIX.

Soon as great Puritàn's parental care
Wants physical, all infant needs supplied,
He intellectual culture 'gan prepare;
And most of all the morals sought to guide;
Religious training zealous to provide,
Made lawful, dangerous espionage;
Aye strengthen'd innate germs of selfish pride;
The very ills he sought by flight to assuage,
Shall these perpetuate, and e'en their friends enrage?

XXX.

Is this a Zion, where the saints alone
Shall enter?   Who can tell the constant care
Of every soul, that there shall not be one
Of diverse faith among his followers there;
Who dares to love, or use the written prayer
Who dares to think, much less to speak a word,
His solemn covenant doth not declare
To him, no rest this haven may afford!
All must believe as he believes, or be abhorred—

XXXI.

Be driven back across the raging Sea,
Or cast amid the howling wilderness!
And many felt his arm fall heavily,
For he was stern, and proud, and strong t' impress
His will with energy and stubbornness;
And held denial of his ghostly power
Political hostility: unless
Faith uniform prevailed, the ills that lower
O'er other lands, might here arise in fatal hour

XXXII.

Freedom and sanctity of conscience right?
Right, to permit men to believe and teach
Error?   Shall God's own chosen tolerate
Sin and foul heresy?   These will impeach
Who shall declare the liberty of each
To his own faith; the *truth* all must believe;
Taught by the faithful, nor with wanton speech
Attempt defense, the souls of saints to grieve,
They must at least profess belief, whom these receive.

XXXIII.

Know ye Rogerus? Never nobler soul
Dwelt in the bosom of a mortal man;
Not that chivalrous knight poets extol,
Who fought and conquered under Charlemagne,
Wedded to Britomartis, whence began
A mighty race of kings; braver than he—
A noble compeer this, of Puritàn—
Whom he had loved and served and faithfully
Followed from far, still fond to serve chivalrously.

XXXIV.

Avaunt, Rogerus! Is the world not wide?
Disturb them not with new unwonted light;
Hence Aquiday!   No knight shall here abide
Who is not meek and faithful: hence Wheelright,
And Aspinwall, hence Coddington, what right
Hast thou to brave this knight despitefully?
Wenlock, Dyer, Leddra, Marmaduke invite
Sentence of death; in vain he bids them fly,
They vow t' abide, and by his hand die wretchedly.

XXXV.

But farthest followers of his Godly faith
Found succor at his hands; his care extends
O'er far Connecticut; he saves from wrath
Far as Lygonia, Gorgeana, lends
His aid: he Agamenticus defends,
And his own Plymouth, ever near and dear;
And from his growing people proudly sends
Succor to England, when his brethren there,
The doom of kings and prelates wrath are forced to bear.

XXXVI.

Thus was achieved his onerous enterprise;
He led the van across the mighty deep;
He roused the nation's latent energies,
Giving an impulse that should never sleep,
For myriad souls, the vigils hence should keep.
The many villages he planted there,
Strong arms, the mighty wilderness to sweep
With power away, nor savages to spare,
In earnest struggles these 'gainst nature bring to bear.

XXXVII.

This work of human hands—by dauntless will
Encouraged and directed, fills the world
With wonder; far-off nations gazing still,
To mark how Puritanic race has hurled
The gauntlet of achievement, and unfurled
Its standard, Liberty, with power and pride!
Where human progress all the past has purled,
Here an advancing flood—deep, swift, and wide—
What can withstand the power of the willful tide?

XXXVIII.

Who can predict results? He who can stand
Upon the extremest verge of time, and gaze
From *then* to *now* on changes in this land,
May shrink from all predictions; naught can raise
The veil of dark futurity, that lays
E'en o'er to-morrow; who now dares conceive
What will be, when two centuries long maze
Have crystallized in facts; sure ye believe
With much to praise, vast changes may bring much to grieve.

13

XXXIX.

Be wise, Oh nation! Power for weal or woe
Dwells in the bosom of each citizen;
Past history doth clearly to thee show
Th' undisciplined fierce passions of past men;
Will not *each* curb *his* dangerous passions then?
Priceless experience of all mankind—
When will man learn its worth? Oh when, Oh when?
Blest is the nation that doth early find
To learn from others' woes, ere passion makes it blind!

www.ingramcontent.com/pod-product-compliance
Lightning Source LLC
Chambersburg PA
CBHW020033030726
47499CB00007B/2405